Enid Blyton

The Adventures of Binkle & Flip

Enid Blyton

The Adventures of Binkle & Flip

Happy Days

BBounty
BOOKS

First published in 1938.

This edition published in 2013 by Bounty Books,
a division of Octopus Publishing Group Ltd,
Endeavour House,
189 Shaftesbury Avenue,
London WC2H 8JY
www.octopusbooks.co.uk

An Hachette UK Company
www.hachette.co.uk
Enid Blyton ® Text copyright © 1938, 2013 Hodder & Stoughton Ltd.
Illustrations copyright © 2013 Octopus Publishing Group Ltd.
Layout copyright © 2013 Octopus Publishing Group Ltd.

Illustrated by Stephen Dell.
Cover illustration by Alan Fredman.

ISBN: 978-0-75372-580-1

A CIP catalogue record for this book is available from the British Library.

Printed and bound in India by Manipal Technologies Ltd, Manipal

Contents

Stories

Poems

Bad
Bunnies

Let me introduce you to a
    Bad
        Bold
            Pair,
They live in Heather Cottage and you'll
Find
    Them
        There,
They're Flip and Binkle Bunny, and I
Think
    You'll
        Decide,
They're the biggest rascals ever met, since
Brer
    Rabbit
        Died!

And now I'll tell of Oak Tree Town with
All
    Its
        Folks,
On whom the rascal pair of bunnies
Play
    Such
        Jokes,
There's Dilly Duck and Derry Dormouse,
Sharp,
    Riggles
        Rat,
Mowdie Mole and Herbert Hedgehog
Prickled
    And
        Fat.
Robert Rabbit, Sammy Squirrel,
Wee
    Mary
        Mouse,
And Brock the Badger, Chimney-sweep for
Each
    One's
        House

Then Wily Weasel, who's a policeman,
And,
    Sad
        To Tell,
He sometimes catches Flip and Binkle
And
    Scolds
        Them Well!
There is no time to tell you more
Of Oak
    Tree
        Town,
But if you read these tales you'll find it's
All
    Written
        Down.
And there you'll find the many tricks,
Quaint,
    Clever,
        Funny,
Of both those imps of naughtiness,
FLIP
    AND BINKLE
        BUNNY!

Chapter 1
Flip's New Job

Flip and Binkle Bunny were walking down Acorn Street when they came to the baker's shop. Derry Dormouse the baker was inside cooking, and a perfectly lovely smell came from the hot cakes he was baking.

Binkle stood still and sniffed.

'My,' he said, 'that smells, good! Got any money, Flip!'

'You know I haven't!' said Flip. 'I spent my last penny yesterday.'

'And I haven't any either,' said Binkle, sadly pressing his nose against the window and looking at all the lovely things inside.

'No one will give us a job,' wailed Flip, 'so I expect we shall starve! Oh dear!'

Suddenly Binkle caught sight of a little notice pinned up near the door. He went over to it and read it.

Then he scratched his head, leaned against the window, and thought hard.

'What is it, Binkle?' asked Flip, astonished to see his friend thinking so deeply.

'Sh! Wait a moment. I've got an idea,' said Binkle, beginning to look excited. 'Come and read this notice, Flip.'

Flip went up and looked at the notice. It was very short and neat.

WANTED

A quiet and clever nursemaid for four baby foxes. Please apply to
Furry Fox
Mossy Bank, Cuckoo Wood.

'Well, I don't see anything in that notice to get excited about,' he said. 'We're not nursemaids! And I'm sure I wouldn't want to go and look after four sly little fox babies, even if I *was* a nurse!'

'Oh, you never think of anything!' said Binkle. 'You haven't got any brains at all, Flip! Look here! What about dressing-up as a nursemaid and going to see if we can get the job?'

'Gracious, Binkle, are you mad?' gasped Flip, sitting down suddenly on Derry's doorstep. 'Furry Fox is fierce enough to *eat* us if she found us out in a trick like that!'

'But why *should* she find us out?' argued Binkle. 'I can borrow some of my sister's clothes, and one of us can easily dress up. Old Furry Fox and her husband Fatty are rich enough to pay good wages, and four silly little fox-cubs would be easy enough to look after.'

'Well, *you* can do the dressing-up,' said Flip firmly, standing up again. 'I'm not going to have anything to do with such a foolish and dangerous idea.' And he walked off with his head in the air.

'Flip!' called Binkle, running after him. 'Don't be mean! Help me to dress up, then! Come on to Bess Bunny's house with me, and see if she'll lend us some clothes.'

Well, Flip didn't mind doing that, and he went off with Binkle to call on Bess Bunny, Binkle's sister, who lived in Bramble Dell just outside Oak Tree Town.

They knocked at the door. Blim-blam, blim-blam!

Bess opened it. She was a thin, rather worried-looking rabbit, for she had a large family of children. She wasn't very pleased to see Binkle and Flip, for they had a bad name in Oak Tree Town.

'What do you want?' she asked, when they were inside. 'You don't generally come and see me unless you want something.'

'I've brought you a present!' said Binkle in a hurt tone, putting a little bunch of pretty berries down on the table. 'We picked these for you, knowing how much you liked flowers and bright berries, for your dinner table.'

Bess looked pleased.

'Well, thank you, I'm sure,' she said, putting them in water.

'That's a new dress you're wearing, isn't it?' asked Binkle, looking at it very admiringly.

'Yes, it is,' answered Bess. 'My old one was getting so shabby!'

'Oh, that reminds me, Bess,' said Binkle. 'Could you lend me your old dress for a little while? I'd take great care of it.'

'What in the world for?' said Bess, in astonishment. 'Are you going to a fancy-dress party?'

'Well, not exactly that,' said Binkle. 'Something in that line, though.'

Flip giggled. 'You won't get Bess to lend you her old frock to go to a fancy-dress party in,' he chuckled.

'Oh, *won't* he!' snapped Bess, turning round and glaring at Flip, whom she disliked. 'Well, you're wrong. I *will* lend it to him.'

She ran out of the room to fetch it.

'That was a very clever remark of yours,' whispered Binkle to Flip, who looked most astonished, for he hadn't meant to be clever at all.

Bess came back with her old striped dress and a small red shawl.

'Here you are,' she said; 'it's quite neat and tidy. Oh, and here's the bonnet to go with it.'

'Oh, that's fine!' said Binkle gratefully. 'You are a dear, Bess; we'll take it straight away, now.'

Bess wrapped up the things for them, said goodbye, and saw them off. Binkle was tremendously pleased. He rushed off to his cottage on Bumble Bee Common at such a pace that Flip could hardly keep up with him.

But what a disappointment when he tried the things on! They didn't fit him at all! For Binkle was plump and round, and Bessie's clothes didn't meet anywhere on him! Her little bonnet on his large head looked perfectly ridiculous. He was terribly disappointed.

'Here, you try them on, Flip!' he said at last.

So Flip, who was small and rather thin, slipped on Bessie's striped frock. It fitted him perfectly! Binkle draped the little red shawl over his shoulders and pinned it in front. Then he perched the bonnet on Flip's head – and my, he looked as like a nurse-maid as you could wish!

'Flip, you look fine!' cried Binkle. 'Look at yourself in the glass. You *must* go to Furry Fox and see if she'll take you as a nursemaid.'

Flip looked at himself. Certainly no one would think he was Bad Flip Bunny, well known all over Oak Tree Town for the naughty pranks he and Binkle were always up to.

'You would make a splendid nursemaid!' coaxed Binkle, who didn't want his lovely new idea to come to nothing.

Well, after a lot of argument, Flip at last said he would try. So Binkle marched him off to Mossy Bank and watched him go inside the gate and knock at the front door.

Poor Flip was dreadfully nervous. He didn't like the Fox family, for it was said that old Fatty Fox enjoyed a meal of rabbit pie when he could get it.

Furry Fox opened the door.

'Please,' said Flip, 'I saw your notice about wanting a nursemaid.'

'Oh, come in,' said Furry Fox.

Flip stepped inside. He saw four small fox cubs sitting in a row by the kitchen fire, all sucking comforters and looking as good as gold.

'Have you looked after babies before!' asked Furry.

'No, ma'am, but I think I could,' answered Flip nervously.

'Huh, you don't sound as if you know much about it!' sniffed Furry Fox, scornfully. 'I don't think you'll do.'

Just at that moment Fatty Fox came in. He stopped short at the sight of the little rabbit.

'Ha! A new nursemaid!' he cried. 'She looks fine, Wife! I hope you've engaged her!'

Furry looked at him, and saw by the look in his eyes that he thought Flip might come in useful for a pie. She smiled.

'Well, I think we'll try you for a little!' she said to Flip. 'You can stay with us until Christmas, at any rate. That's just a fortnight. And I'll pay you a pound a day.'

Flip was very pleased to hear that. A pound a day seemed a great deal. He would be quite rich at the end of two weeks.

'Thank you, ma'am,' he said.

Furry Fox told him to look after the fox babies whilst she and her husband went out. So Flip settled down by the fire with the babies, and as soon as the two foxes had gone, he took his pipe out of a pocket and began to fill it.

'Hist!' whispered a voice from the window, making Flip jump nearly out of his skin. He turned round and saw Binkle peeping through.

'Don't light your pipe, you stupid! That will give everything away! Nursemaids don't smoke!'

Flip put his pipe away hurriedly, and began to tell Binkle how he had got the job for a fortnight at a pound a day. Binkle was delighted.

'My word!' he chuckled. 'We'll have a fine time after Christmas, spending the money, won't we?'

'Yes, but I don't like the job much!' said Flip. 'Can't smoke, can't sleep when I want to, and can't wear my own clothes!'

'Oh never mind,' comforted Binkle. 'You'll get on perfectly all right.'

But that's just where he was wrong. Flip got on very badly.

To begin with, *he* didn't know how to amuse babies. He didn't even know how to carry them. They squealed whenever he picked them up. And they had sharp teeth too, as Flip found out one morning when he was trying his hardest to dress the biggest baby. She didn't want her bonnet put on, so she set her teeth into Flip's paw, and my, didn't he jump!

'Ow! You little nuisance!' he cried, and shouted loudly at her.

You should have heard her howl! Furry Fox came running in to see whatever the matter was, and gave Flip a scolding for daring to upset one of her precious babies.

'Well, I'm not going to be bitten,' grumbled Flip under his breath.

'You'll be bitten harder still soon!' thought Furry Fox, thinking of Christmas and rabbit pie.

Every night Furry gave Flip, a round shiny pound, and he put it away in his pocket, feeling very pleased indeed to hear them jingle away there. A whole week went by, and Flip had seven pounds. He thought how pleased Binkle would be when he told him how rich he was getting.

Then after a few days something dreadful happened. Flip went out for a walk with the fox-babies well strapped into their pram – and he came back with only *three* babies!

Furry met him at the door and was just going to ask if any of the babies had been to sleep, when she saw one was missing.

'Where is Fluffy?' she cried. 'What have you done with Fluffy? Have you lost him?'

Flip looked down at the babies and saw there were only three.

'Oh my!' he cried, in dismay. 'There's only three! *I* don't know what's happened to Fluffy!'

Furry Fox flew into a dreadful rage and caught poor Flip by the ear.

'Tell me what you've done with Fluffy or I'll eat you!' she cried.

Flip dropped down on his knees.

'Please have mercy!' he sobbed. 'I don't know, really. He must have dropped out of the pram when I wasn't looking. I'm terribly sorry.'

'Fine nursemaid *you* are!' snorted Furry, catching hold of him by the wrist. 'Come along. You're going to take me exactly where you've been with the babies, and see if we can find poor little Fluffy. If we can't – well!' and she glared at Flip so fiercely that he shook all over and his ears went floppy.

Furry dragged him through the wood, but though they looked everywhere for Fluffy, they couldn't see any sign of him.

So, growling with anger, Furry Fox dragged Flip home again, saying that she would tell her husband, Fatty, all about it. When they got to Mossy Bank, the three babies were playing in the yard. Furry counted them, snorted, and took Flip indoors, to call Fatty.

But directly they got indoors, Furry pricked up her ears. She heard something squealing upstairs.

And there on his cot in the nursery lay Fluffy, squealing for Furry!

'Oh! I must have forgotten to put him in the pram with the others!' said Flip suddenly. 'I left him behind by mistake. So if I only took three babies out, I could only bring three babies back, couldn't I, Mistress Fox?'

Furry glared at him.

'I don't believe you're a nursemaid at all!' she cried.

'Well, I'm *not*,' said Flip unexpectedly. 'And I'm tired of your silly babies, so there. I'm Flip Bunny and I'm going home!'

He turned to go – but Furry caught hold of him.

'Oho!' she said. 'So you've been playing a trick on us, have you? All right! We'll play

23

one on *you*!' and catching him by the scruff of his neck, she dragged him into a little room nearby and shut the door on him. He heard the click of the key turning in the lock, and he ran to the window. Alas! it was barred.

'That *was* a silly idea of Binkle's to dress up as a nursemaid,' he said. 'Suppose Furry and Fatty decide to eat me! How *can* I get away?'

He stayed there all day, very lonely and miserable. But when night came, he heard a noise of stones being thrown against his window. He peeped out between the bars.

'Hist!' came Binkle's voice. 'I was behind a tree when Furry went through the wood this morning, holding you by your neck. What's the matter?'

Flip told him.

'You must get away as quickly as possible,' said Binkle.

'I can't,' said poor Flip. 'The door's locked and the window is barred.'

Binkle thought for a minute.

'I've got a plan,' he said at last. 'Listen. I will rescue you. I'll do it this way. Are you listening, Flip?'

'Yes, rather!' said Flip.

'You must tell Furry that you've had a letter from Santa Claus to say he's bringing the fox babies presents on Christmas Eve,' said Binkle. 'Say he'll drive up to the front door and jingle his bells for you to come down and get the presents. Then we'll race off together and you'll be safe!'

Flip agreed to the plan, although he didn't really believe it would be much good. Binkle wrote a letter, tied a stone round it, and threw it up to Flip. It said:

I will come on Christmas Eve and bring presents for the Fox Babies.

Santa Claus.

Next morning, Furry came into Flip's room, but before she could say anything Flip pushed the letter into her hand.

'Look!' he said, pretending to be excited. 'I know Santa Claus, so I expect he'll bring some lovely presents! This letter came in at the window last night.'

Furry Fox thought it was rather wonderful. She went out of the room to show Fatty the letter. Presently she came back.

'You can stay here till Christmas,' she said, 'and get the presents from Santa Claus.' Then she went out again and banged the door and locked it.

'And on Christmas Day you think you'll have me for dinner!' said Flip, chuckling. 'But you won't.'

Two days went by, and then Christmas Eve came. The fox babies were very excited to think Santa Claus was coming. Fatty and Furry kept a watch out, too, but the night was much too dark for them to see anybody coming.

Binkle was creeping up through the darkness. When he came to Mossy Bank, he took some little bells out of his pocket and tied them on to the branch of a tree. The wind blew them, and they tinkled like sleigh-bells.

'Santa Claus! – Santa Claus!' cried the babies.

Then a deep voice came out of the darkness.

'I am here! Do not keep me waiting!'

Furry took Flip and pushed him out of the front door. He ran out, and bumped into Binkle. Then he twisted his skirts up out of the way of his legs and *ran* for his life through Cuckoo Wood with Binkle.

Furry and Fatty waited and waited. They heard the bells tinkling in the wind and thought that Santa Claus was still there, talking to Flip.

'What a lot of presents he must be giving!' whispered Furry.

But Fatty grew suspicious. At last he ran out into the darkness and called to Flip. But there was no answer! Flip was far away. Then

Fatty's head bumped into the tinkling bells, and he knew it was all a trick.

How angry they all were!

'And he's got ten pounds of ours!' snarled Furry. 'And we haven't any Christmas dinner!'

For their Christmas dinner was away in Heather Cottage on Bumble Bee Common, dressing himself in his own old clothes and smoking his pipe.

And with the ten pounds Flip and Binkle bought a lovely Christmas dinner – and my, didn't they enjoy it!

'No more dressing-up for me!' sighed Flip, as he ate a large mince pie. 'It's too danger-ous. *I* don't want to be anybody's Christmas dinner, I can tell you. I was lucky to get off as well as I did.'

And I really think he *was*, don't you?

Chapter 2

Binkle Has the Doctor

'I'm going down to Oak Tree Town to buy a stamp, Flip,' said Binkle. 'Are you coming?'

'Yes,' said Flip, reaching for his cap, 'I'm ready.'

Off the two trotted over Bumble Bee Common, down Hazel Road into Oak Tree Town.

But when they got to the post office, it was shut!

'Shut!' said Binkle in amazement. 'Shut! At eleven o'clock in the morning too! Fine sort of postmistress Dilly Duck is!'

Just at that moment someone walked up to the post office door.

'Mind, please!' said a little voice. 'I want to go in.'

'But it's shut,' said Binkle, turning round and seeing Timothy Mouse. He was carrying a steaming basin covered with a cloth.

'Of course it's shut!' said Timothy. 'Dilly's very ill. I'm taking her some soup my mother's made. Doesn't it smell good!'

And he went inside the post office and shut the door.

No sooner had he gone than someone else came up, carrying a big pink jelly on a dish.

'Good morning, Mowdie Mole,' said Binkle politely. 'Are you taking that to Dilly Duck?'

'Yes, I am. She's ill,' answered Mowdie, going into the shop.

Binkle and Flip stared at each other and sighed.

'Jelly and soup!' said Flip sadly. 'We never have those, Binkle.'

'And here's some flowers and grapes!' sighed Binkle, seeing Herbert Hedgehog coming up the street with his arms full.

The two rabbits went slowly home.

'Isn't it a pity one of us can't be a *little* bit ill!' said Flip.

Binkle stopped suddenly.

'That's a great idea of yours,' he said. 'One of us *will* be ill.'

'We can't be,' said Flip. 'We're both as well as can be, Binkle. Don't be silly!'

'I'm *not* silly,' said Binkle. 'I'm thinking about our idea.'

'It isn't our idea, Binkle,' groaned Flip. 'I don't have ideas. They're dangerous!'

But it was no use. Binkle was already making plans.

'Now shall you be ill, or shall I?' he wondered.

'*I'm* not going to be,' said Flip firmly, 'and I won't help *you* to be either, Binkle, and I mean that!'

'Fiddlesticks!' said Binkle rudely. 'You'll do just as I tell you, Flip. But you needn't be the ill one. I will; I should love that.'

'Oh dear! Very well, *be* ill!' said Flip desperately, and they went into Heather Cottage.

'I won't be ill *just* yet,' Binkle said – 'not till Dilly's better, anyway. People can't take broth and jelly to two people at once. I'll wait for a bit and think about it.'

He waited for a week and then heard that Dilly was up and about again.

'Now's the time!' he said.

He undressed and got into bed. Flip put a clean bed cover on, and made the room look as tidy as possible.

'Oh! Oh! Oh!' groaned Binkle in bed, rolling his eyes and opening and shutting his mouth.

'What's the matter?' asked Flip, in alarm.

'Nothing! I'm only just seeing if I can be ill properly,' grinned Binkle, tying a piece of red flannel round his neck. 'Now, Flip, you must do your part.'

'Part? What part?' asked Flip, his nose going up and down nervously. 'I'm not doing anything this time, Binkle.'

'Oh yes, you are,' said Binkle firmly. 'You're going to go to Sammy Squirrel the chemist, and ask him what's the best thing for a Shivering Fever.'

'Shivering Fever! I never heard of *that*!' said Flip.

'Nor have I,' chuckled Binkle. 'He'll ask you all about it, and you can say what you like. Say I've got headaches and a cold, and I'm hot and I'm shivering and I can't sleep!'

'Oh, Binkle, you're perfectly awful!' sighed poor Flip, putting on his coat. He went off, shaking his head, and wishing that Binkle wouldn't always be wanting to behave so badly.

He went to Sammy Squirrel's. There were a lot of people in the shop, but at last he got his turn.

'What's the best thing for a Shivering Fever?' he asked Sammy.

'Shivering Fever!' exclaimed Sammy. 'What's that? Who's got it?'

'Binkle has!' explained Flip. 'He's cold and he's hot and he's got headaches.'

'Headaches! How many headaches has he got?' enquired Sammy with a grin.

'He's got two,' answered Flip sharply. 'One at the front and one at the back.'

'I'm sorry to hear that,' said kind Dilly Duck. 'I've just been ill myself, so I know how horrid it is. After you've got the medicine you want from Sammy, come in to me, next door, Flip, and I'll give you a jelly to take to Binkle.'

Sammy gave Flip a bottle of medicine to be taken three times a day. Then Flip ran in to the post office and Dilly gave him a yellow jelly in a big mould.

'Come and tell me how he is tomorrow,' she said. 'Has he had the doctor?'

'Er – no,' answered Flip. 'He says he won't see the doctor.'

'Dear, dear, dear, what a pity!' said Dilly, and when Flip had gone she went into Sammy's shop again and told him that Binkle wouldn't see a doctor.

'He may get terribly ill,' she said.

'Don't you worry, Dilly,' grinned Sammy. 'Binkle isn't ill, he's only pretending. Why, I saw him yesterday looking as well as ever I've seen him!'

'But, Sammy, supposing he *is* ill,' said Gillie Guinea-pig. 'It would be horrid not to be nice to him, even if he is always up to tricks, and behaves so badly.'

'Yes, he's a bad bunny, but if he's ill we *ought* to be nice to him – I quite agree with Gillie,' said Mowdie Mole.

Sammy thought for a minute, then his eyes twinkled.

'I'll find out for you!' he promised. 'I'll pretend I'm a doctor, and I'll go and find out. If he is really ill, we'll do our best to be kind. If he isn't – well, we'll see!'

Flip would have felt rather uncomfortable if he had known what Sammy was planning. But he didn't know – so he went on towards Heather Cottage, carrying the jelly carefully, and occasionally giving it a lick, just to see if it tasted good.

'Well?' said Binkle, when Flip came into the bedroom. 'What has happened?'

'*This* happened!' said Flip proudly, holding up the jelly. 'It's lovely! I've licked it, to see!'

The two rabbits soon finished up the jelly between them, and Flip told Binkle all that had happened. Binkle was very pleased.

'I expect lots of people will come and bring nice things,' he said hopefully. 'Do I look nice, Flip?'

'You look all right,' said Flip. 'What you've got to do isn't to look *nice*, though – you've got to look *ill*.'

Nobody else called that day, and Binkle was rather disappointed.

But the next day there came a terrific rat-tat-tat on the door.

'There's somebody,' chuckled Binkle. 'Go and see who it is, Flip.'

Flip opened the door. It was someone dressed in a smart suit and coat, and a black hat. In his paw he carried a bag.

Flip stared at him in surprise.

'I'm Doctor Curemquick,' smiled the visitor. 'Sammy Squirrel told me to come and look you up. Someone's very ill here, isn't he?'

Poor Flip didn't know what in the world to say!

'Well, Binkle isn't very well,' he stammered at last. 'He's upstairs in bed.'

'I'll go up and see him,' said the doctor, and pushing past Flip, he ran upstairs.

He walked into the bedroom and went

across to the bed. Binkle stared at him in astonishment.

'It's the doctor, Binkle,' said Flip, who had followed close behind the visitor.

'I didn't ask any doctor to come and see me,' growled Binkle, twitching his ears nervously.

'No, Sammy Squirrel asked me to come,' said the doctor cheerfully. 'Now then, let's have a look at you! Put out your tongue!'

Binkle put out a very pink little tongue. The doctor looked at it and shook his head.

'Dear me!' he said, taking out a little note-book and writing something. 'Dear Me!'

'What's the matter?' asked Binkle in alarm.

'Now take a deep breath,' said the doctor, without answering Binkle's question.

Binkle took a deep breath and the doctor tapped him hard on the chest.

'Don't do that!' said Binkle. 'You hurt me.'

'Now flap your ears up and down,' ordered the doctor, writing busily again.

Binkle did so, feeling very nervous indeed at the sight of the doctor's grave face. He began to be afraid there really must be something terribly wrong with him.

'Dear me – dear me!' said the doctor. 'A very sad case – a – very – sad – case!'

'What's the matter with him?' asked Flip miserably, terribly upset to hear Binkle was really ill.

'Fiddle-faddlitis!' answered the doctor. 'I'll send him some medicine and some pills, and something to rub his chest with. He mustn't get up and he mustn't read. He must just lie quietly in bed and do nothing.'

'What shall I give him to eat?' asked Flip. 'Jellies and things?'

'Good gracious me, no!' said the doctor. 'Jellies and soups and things like that would kill him, in his state of health. Feed him on

39

carrot-tops mashed fine, and nothing else.
I'll call again in a few days.'

He ran downstairs and out of the house.
All the way over Bumble Bee Common he
chuckled and chortled to himself.

'I knew he was shamming,' he said. 'This
will teach him to pretend to be ill. My, what a
tale to tell the others!'

And when Oak Tree Town heard how
Sammy Squirrel had dressed up as a doctor
and gone to see Binkle, you should have
seen them smile!

But Binkle and Flip weren't smiling.

'No jellies! No soups! No broths! What's
the *good* of being ill?' groaned Binkle.
'Carrot-tops minced fine! Ugh!'

'Yes, this is what comes of pretending to
be ill!' scolded Flip. 'If you hadn't pretended, you wouldn't really be!'

'Don't be silly!' said Binkle, feeling that he
was showing very little sympathy. 'I feel very
bad, so there! Oh! Oh! Oh!'

'Don't, Binkle!' begged Flip, who was
really very upset to hear Binkle was ill. 'I
can't bear it. I'll do all I can for you, you
know that. I'll go and get some carrot-tops
this very minute.'

But before he could do that, all the medicine came. Such an array there was! Boxes and bottles and jars!

Binkle tried them all. He was really afraid something was the matter with him, and he felt he ought to do all that the doctor had said.

But ugh, the medicine tasted dreadful! The pills tasted worse! And as for the stuff to rub on his chest – well, it smelt terrible!

Poor Binkle groaned and sighed, ate his carrot-tops and took his medicines. He didn't dare to get up, but just lay still in his bed as the doctor had ordered, feeling duller and duller each day.

Days passed, and no doctor came. Binkle had finished all the medicine and pills, and felt as if he never wanted to see a bottle again in his life.

'What's that doctor doing?' he groaned. 'Flip, go down to Sammy Squirrel's and ask him when Doctor Curemquick's coming again.'

Flip went – but, to his great astonishment, Sammy didn't seem to know anything about the doctor.

'Doctor Curemquick? Who *is* he?' he

asked. 'He's never been heard of in Oak Tree Town before!'

'Well, you didn't send him, then?' gasped Flip. 'What an extraordinary thing! And poor old Binkle's been taking his medicine and pills every day, and they were as nasty as could be!'

'Has he finished them?' asked Sammy Squirrel, chuckling loudly.

'Yes, every one,' said Flip. 'What are you laughing at, Sammy?'

'Oh, just thoughts,' answered Sammy, chuckling still more loudly. 'Just my thoughts, Flip. They're rather funny!'

Flip's nose went up and down angrily.

'I believe you know more about Doctor Curemquick than you want to tell me!' he said, and stalked out of the shop and back to Bumble Bee Common.

He told Binkle that Sammy seemed to know nothing about the doctor.

'And Sammy seemed to think you being ill and having to drink medicine was a tremendous joke,' he ended.

'Oh! *Oh!* OH!' yelled Binkle, suddenly jumping out of bed with a tremendous leap. 'Well, of course it was a joke! A joke! Oh, my stars! It must have been Sammy who dressed up as the doctor. I thought his face seemed a bit familiar!'

Flip's eyes opened wide.

'And he sent you all that nasty medicine – and made you stay in bed – and said you weren't to have jellies and soups!' he said. Then he suddenly began to laugh.

'It's – it's – it's very f-f-funny, Binkle,' he said, between his gurgles of laughter. 'You pretended to be ill – and Sammy pretended you were ill – and you thought you were and you weren't! Oh my!'

And he went off into peals of laughter again.

'Be quiet, Flip,' growled Binkle, beginning to dress himself. 'It isn't at all funny. It's a very horrid trick. It's very wrong of Sammy to pretend like that.'

'But *you* began it first,' went on Flip, chuckling loudly.

'Well, I shan't pretend any more,' roared Binkle. 'And if you don't stop laughing, I won't talk to you, so there!'

But though Flip stopped laughing, Oak Tree Town didn't.

And you can't think how red Binkle got when anyone he met asked him if he was *really* better!

Chapter 3

Binkle's Wonderful Picture

Binkle woke up one morning and tried to remember a dream he had had. He stared up at the ceiling and thought. It had been a very nice dream – he had done something that everyone admired – now, what was it?

'I know!' he cried suddenly, banging the bedclothes. 'I painted a wonderful picture!'

'Binkle,' shouted Flip angrily, waking up with a jump, 'stop hitting me!'

'You shouldn't be so near me, then,' said Binkle. 'Listen, Flip, to my wonderful dream. I dreamed I painted a marvellous picture of Oak Tree Town, and I dreamed that Rombo, the famous painter-rabbit came and told me it was the best picture he had ever seen. Fancy that!'

'What was the picture like?' asked Flip, very interested.

'That's the funny part,' said Binkle, frowning. 'However much I looked at it, I couldn't seem to see any picture at all. But everybody else did.'

'H'm – rather a silly dream,' said Flip, suddenly feeling sleepy again, and began to snore before Binkle could tell him any more.

But Binkle went on thinking about it, until, half awake and half asleep, he found himself smiling over an absurd idea that had just occurred to him. He gave a chuckle.

'I'll do it,' he said, 'and see what happens.'

He went on planning until he had everything clear in his mind. Then he woke Flip up and told him what he was going to do.

'Don't be silly, Binkle!' said Flip. 'You must be half asleep to think of a thing like that.'

'I'm very much awake, thank you,' said Binkle, and tweaked Flip's nose, so that he squealed in anger and sat up to pummel Binkle.

But Binkle was already out of bed. 'That's right, Flip,' he chuckled. 'I thought that would wake you up.'

The two rabbits dressed quickly and got

their breakfast. Whilst they were having it, Binkle told Flip what he was to do that morning, and gave him a long list of things to buy.

'And mind you tell everyone I'm going to paint a wonderful picture,' he ended.

Off went Flip to buy paintbrushes, paints, canvas, an easel, and a palette. He bought them all, but wouldn't let them be wrapped up. He wanted everyone to see them.

Carrying them all carefully, he went slowly down the street, meeting Herbert Hedgehog, Dilly Duck, Derry Dormouse, and Riggles Rat, and many others who were doing their morning shopping.

'Goodness gracious!' they all cried, as one by one they met him. 'What in the world are you going to do, Flip Bunny?'

'I'm just taking these home to Binkle,' Flip told everyone. 'He's got an idea for a wonderful picture. Oak Tree Town will be proud of it, I can tell you!'

'Fiddlesticks!' grunted Herbert Hedgehog. 'You can't make *me* believe Binkle can paint.'

'You don't know *what* Binkle can do,' answered Flip. 'You just wait and see his picture, Herbert.'

Well, of course, all Oak Tree Town was very interested in Binkle's new work. They didn't quite know what to think about it. Binkle was a surprising Bunny, and nobody ever knew what he would do next.

So everybody talked about his painting and wondered how it was getting on and whether anyone would be allowed to see it. Which was just what Binkle wanted them to do.

Binkle was very busy. He had found a nice sheltered spot in the garden, and here he had put up his easel and canvas. He had also brought out his little stool and all his brushes and paints. He mixed a little of each colour on his enormous palette and thought it looked very artistic indeed.

But he didn't put a single dab of paint on his canvas. That was left quite empty.

Then he sent Flip into the woods with a spade and told him to dig up any old roots he could see, and if anyone asked him what he wanted, to say that he was taking Blue Fuzzymuz, Red Rillobies, and Purple Pittitoos for Binkle to mix with his paints.

'But why?' asked Flip, most astonished.

'To make my picture magic!' answered Binkle, with a chuckle.

So off went Flip with a sack and dug up bluebell roots and violet roots.

Riggles Rat saw him doing it, and wanted to know why.

'I'm taking Blue Fuzzymuz, Red Rillobies, and Purple Pittitoos to Binkle,' answered Flip. 'He mixes them with his paints, you know, and they make his picture magic.'

'How?' asked Riggles, amazed.

'I don't quite know yet,' answered Flip truthfully, going on his way with the heavy sack. 'Tell you tomorrow, p'raps.'

Riggles was most curious. 'Come to tea

with me tomorrow,' he cried, 'and tell me all about it.'

'Right!' said Flip and went off.

He told Binkle about his meeting with Riggles, and Binkle laughed till he cried.

'Go and put those old roots in the shed,' he said, 'and then come back and I'll tell you what to say to him.'

When Flip came back, Binkle took him to his easel in the garden.

'What do you see there!' he asked, pointing to the empty canvas.

'Nothing,' answered Flip, rather astonished.

'Well, listen,' said Binkle solemnly. 'I'm painting a picture there that only *clever* people can see. Stupid ones won't see anything at all. It's magic, you see. My dream gave me the idea. When the picture's finished, we'll let people in to see it at twenty pence a time!'

Flip stared at him. He wished he hadn't said he could see nothing. Then something in Binkle's smile made him ask a question.

'Binkle,' he said, 'are you *really* painting a picture?'

'No, not really,' chuckled Binkle. 'But I

don't expect anyone will like to say so, in case we think they're stupid. We'll just see how many people we take in, Flip. But I'm going to get Rombo the painter-rabbit to say it's wonderful first.'

'Rombo! But he'd never come. And he'd say you hadn't painted a picture at all,' cried Flip.

'Not the real Rombo! I'm going to ask my cousin Rab the Bunny from Bracken Hill Town to dress up and pretend he's Rombo,' chuckled Binkle. 'I've written to ask him to come on Friday. What fun! You must be sure and tell Riggles that, when you go to tea with him tomorrow.'

So next day off went Flip, dressed in his best, to Riggles the Rat. He found that Herbert Hedgehog was there too, and Mowdie Mole, all very eager to hear the latest news of Binkle's painting.

Flip, feeling thoroughly naughty, began to enjoy himself.

'Oh yes,' he said in answer to their questions. 'Binkle's picture is getting on finely. It's a picture of Oak Tree Town and he's putting *everybody* into it!'

'Is he *really*?' said Herbert, most interested,

hoping that he was somewhere well in the front of the picture. 'But isn't there supposed to be something magic about this picture, Flip?'

'Rather!' said Flip. 'He's mixed all sorts of peculiar juices in with his paints – I believe his great-grandmother once told him the secret – and – isn't this strange? – only really clever people can see the picture! Stupid people can't see a thing – it just looks like empty canvas to them!'

Nobody spoke for a minute. They were too astonished and too busy wondering whether they would be able to see this extraordinary picture or not.

Flip went boldly on.

'And Rombo the famous painter-rabbit is coming to see it on Friday,' he said. 'Fancy that!'

'Dear, dear, dear!' said Mowdie Mole, quite breathless with surprise. 'I'd no idea Binkle could paint.'

Nobody could talk of anything else all tea-time but Binkle's wonderful picture. And when Flip went home, he felt quite certain that everyone in Oak Tree Town would know about it before night had fallen. And he was quite right. They did! Mowdie, Riggles, and Herbert saw to that.

Herbert was tremendously excited. He was longing to see the wonderful picture, and longing to know what Rombo said about it. He decided to go up to Binkle's cottage on Friday afternoon and see whether Rombo really had arrived. Riggles said he'd go with him, and Sammy Squirrel too.

So on Friday afternoon all three walked into Binkle's little white gate, and saw Binkle sitting in the garden.

'Good afternoon,' he said kindly. 'I'm so sorry I can't ask you to stay, but I'm expecting Flip to bring Rombo here any minute to see my picture. But do call again afterwards, if you like.'

Rather crossly the three went out again.

'Let's hide here by this tree and hear what Rombo says,' whispered Riggles.

So all three hid silently behind the oak tree that stood next to Binkle's garden. But Binkle was watching out of the corner of his eye and knew quite well they were there. He chuckled to himself.

Presently Flip came up the hill with another rabbit. He was dressed in a black velvet coat and had a long flowing tie and wore very big glasses. Behind both his big ears were stuck lots of paint brushes.

'Oh, good afternoon, Rombo Rabbit,' said Binkle politely. 'It is very good of you to waste your time on me and my picture.'

'Not at all, not at all,' said the make-believe Rombo, who was quite enjoying his part, especially as Flip had promised him a glorious tea afterwards. 'Where is your picture?'

'Here,' said Binkle, leading the way to where his easel stood in the shelter of the bushes.

Rombo peered at it closely. Then he stepped back and looked at it. Then he gazed at it sideways, and finally he went behind it. He came out in front of it again at last, and shook Binkle warmly by the paw.

'Binkle,' he said, 'it's *wonderful!*'

Herbert, Riggles, and Sammy, hidden behind the tree, looked at each other and shook with excitement.

'Did you hear that?' whispered Herbert. 'Binkle's a clever chap!'

'Sh!' said Sammy. 'Rombo's talking again.'

'In fact,' went on Rombo, 'it's *more* than wonderful – it's magic! Magic! Binkle, did you know that?'

'I hoped it might be,' said Binkle modestly.

'Yes,' said Rombo, shaking Binkle by the other paw. 'Mark my words, Binkle Bunny, no stupid person will be able to see that picture of yours. It will only be visible to clever people. Ha! Ha! Now you'll be able to see who's clever and who isn't in Oak Tree Town! Ha! Ha!'

'Ha! Ha!' said Binkle.

'Ha, ha, *ha!*' roared Flip, who had been nearly bursting all the time.

The three hidden behind the oak tree didn't laugh. They were all wondering which of them would be clever enough to see Binkle's picture. Herbert felt *quite* sure he would.

'Better wait here till Rombo's gone,' he whispered. 'Then we'll go and see it.'

The three rascally bunnies were having a glorious tea, and chuckling over the thought of the hidden listeners by the oak tree.

'You did your part well,' said Binkle to Rab, 'but why in the world did you go behind the picture, Rab?'

'He, he! To laugh, of course!' said Rab, stuffing a whole lettuce into his mouth. 'I could see Sammy Squirrel's tail sticking out, and I nearly choked. Ha, ha!'

'Ha, ha!' chuckled Binkle.

'Ha, ha, *ha!*' squealed Flip, who was almost ill with laughing. He never could stop, once he really began.

At last Binkle sent Flip home with Rab. Then he sauntered out into the garden, pulling his lovely whiskers and twitching his big ears. He went to the front gate. Ah! there were Herbert, Riggles, and Sammy Squirrel coming along, all looking rather sheepish.

'May we see your picture now?' asked Herbert.

'Er – well, I was thinking of charging twenty-pence to see it,' said Binkle. 'But I'll let *you* in for nothing, Herbert. The others can see it afterwards if they like to pay twenty-pence.'

'We'll wait and see what Herbert says,' said Sammy cautiously.

So Herbert, feeling very honoured to be let in for nothing, followed Binkle to where his easel stood in the bushes.

When he got there, he stared at the canvas in the greatest dismay – for he couldn't see any picture on it at all!

'That means I'm very stupid!' he thought miserably. 'Dear, dear, dear, and Oak Tree Town has always thought me so clever! I must pretend I see a picture. It must be wonderful if Rombo admired it!'

'Well, what do you think of it?' asked Binkle. 'Do you think the sky is blue enough?'

'Er – er – yes, *quite*!' said Herbert, pretending to look very close. 'Oh yes, decidedly. Oh, it's a wonderful picture, Binkle – wonderful! I shouldn't have thought you could have done it!'

'Oh, it was quite easy,' said Binkle truthfully.

'Er – I'll go and tell Sammy and Riggles to come,' said Herbert, terrified that Binkle might ask him a question he couldn't answer. He hurried to the gate and beckoned to them.

'What's it like?' they asked. 'Is it worth twenty-pence?'

'Oh yes, yes!' said Herbert. 'It's marvellous! Wonderful! Extraordinary! You really must come and see it! It's got a lovely blue sky!'

Well, Sammy and Riggles each paid Binkle twenty-pence and went in. They couldn't believe their eyes when they saw an empty canvas!

'To think old Herbert's clever enough to see it, and I'm not!' thought Sammy Squirrel in great disgust. 'I'm not going to say I can't see it, anyway.'

And Riggles thought just the same, and they began to praise it mightily.

'Finest picture I ever saw,' said Riggles, 'and the blue sky is lovely.'

'Yes, I'm rather pleased with that myself,' said Binkle. 'What do you think of the picture, Sammy?'

Well, Sammy thought a whole lot of things, but he wasn't going to say them. He asked a question.

'Who's that on the left-hand side of the picture?' he asked, pretending to look at it very hard.

'That!' said Binkle in a tone of great surprise. 'Why, that's Herbert! Fancy you not recognising dear old Herbert!'

Herbert bristled all over with importance.

'*I* recognised myself,' he said most untruthfully, 'and it's a *very* good portrait, Binkle!'

'Oh, very!' said Riggles, wishing to goodness *he* could see it.

'Best portrait of the lot, I think,' said Binkle, 'though of course Sammy's very good, too. That's him balancing a nut on his nose. Look,' and he pointed to the right-hand side of the canvas.

How Sammy wished he could see it! It made him feel quite ill, and he thought he'd better go home before the others guessed his stupidity.

The other two said at once that they would go too, and after thanking Binkle very politely for letting them see his masterpiece, they went off down the hill, solemnly talking about Binkle's picture.

'The sky was wonderfully good,' said Herbert.

'It was wonderful,' agreed Riggles.

'But your portrait was lifelike,' said Sammy, determined to keep his end up.

Well, of course, everyone in Oak Tree Town wanted to know what Rombo had said and what the picture was like. All three said it was wonderful and well worth twenty-pence to go and see.

'Of course,' said Sammy, with a laugh, 'you won't all see it, you know! Stupid people can't see a thing! It's a magic sort of picture.'

Everyone was most anxious to go and look at Binkle's picture, and next day the twenty-pences began to pour in.

Dilly Duck came first, and could hardly believe her eyes when she saw nothing on the canvas.

'I always had a sort of feeling I was stupid, and now I know it,' she thought miserably. But aloud she said: 'Yes, yes, yes! A lovely picture! The blue sky is exactly the right colour.'

'Everybody says that,' said Binkle modestly. 'And do you like the trees?'

Dilly looked closely at the canvas and wished heartily she could see what the trees looked like.

'They're *very* nice,' she said, and then suddenly she said she must go home in case anyone wanted stamps. She was afraid Binkle would ask her more questions she couldn't answer. She didn't want him to guess she couldn't see anything.

Mowdie Mole, Susie Squirrel, and Derry Dormouse came, but they didn't stay long. They all said the picture was marvellous, especially the blue sky, and Herbert's portrait, and then they hurried off for fear anyone guessed they were pretending.

Creeper Mouse wanted to know if he could bring his children and Bess Bunny asked if she could bring hers.

'Oh, of course,' answered Binkle, 'but it won't be any use, you know. Children won't be clever enough yet to see my picture. But do bring them!'

So all Bess Bunny's children and Creeper Mouse's family came, and it was just as Binkle had said.

'*I* can't see any pretty picture!' said little Bobbin Bunny.

'I can't see anything!' said wee Mixie Mouse, nearly crying with disappointment.

Of course Bess Bunny and Creeper Mouse couldn't bear to be thought as stupid as their children, so they both said they *loved* the picture and thought it the best they'd ever seen.

Very soon everyone in Oak Tree Town had paid twenty-pence to see Binkle's picture, and all of them, except the children, who really couldn't be expected to be clever enough, said they had seen it, and liked it.

Then Herbert got an idea. He wondered if

Binkle would sell it to him. He thought he would love to have a picture with himself in, especially one that would tell him which of his visitors were clever and which were stupid. So he went up to Heather Cottage and asked Binkle.

'I don't want to *sell* it,' said Binkle. 'I've got a lot of money just now. But I'll give it to you in exchange for six of your biggest cabbages, Herbert Hedgehog.'

Now, Herbert was very proud of his cabbages and he nearly said no. But then he thought of the extraordinary magic of Binkle's picture and he said yes.

'I'll bring the cabbages tonight,' he said, and ran off.

That evening he gave Binkle his six finest cabbages, and received in return Binkle's famous 'picture'. He carried it proudly off and hung it up in the dining-room of his little yellow house.

Everybody was very envious. Whenever they went to call at Herbert's house, he let them have a look at it, and though nobody ever saw anything on the wall but an empty canvas, gradually getting dirty, none of them said anything but: 'Wonderful picture,

Herbert! Wonderful! You're a lucky fellow to have it!'

Now, when Binkle and Flip had eaten all Herbert's cabbages they went to call on him. He was sitting in his cottage, and Dilly, Mowdie Mole, Riggles Rat, and Sammy Squirrel were at tea with him.

'Come in, come in,' called Herbert. 'Very pleased to see our famous artist!'

Binkle and Flip went in and sat down.

'There's your wonderful picture!' said Herbert, waving his pipe towards the wall.

Binkle looked – then he looked again – then he stared hard and rubbed his eyes.

'Herbert,' he said reproachfully, 'you've washed all my picture off the canvas! It's absolutely empty! Isn't it, Flip?'

'Quite,' said Flip. 'Oh, what a pity! Such a lovely picture too! Everybody said how blue the sky was! Oh, Herbert, how could you?'

Herbert looked as if he was going to have a fit. His little eyes grew red and his prickles stood up on end. He couldn't say a word, though he wanted to, terribly badly.

'I'm *surprised* at you, Herbert!' went on Binkle sadly. 'Why did you do it? Oh! I believe I know. You wanted to make people say there was still a picture there, when there wasn't, so that you could laugh up your sleeve at them for pretending, in case anyone thought them stupid! Oh, Herbert, I didn't think it of you! My beautiful picture! All gone! All washed off! Not a trace left!'

Binkle took out his handkerchief, covered his eyes with it, pretended to sob, and walked out of the cottage, followed in a great hurry by Flip, who knew he would have to giggle very soon if he saw Herbert's astonished and indignant face much longer.

As soon as they had gone, Herbert snatched down the picture, broke up the frame, and put the whole thing in the fire. He saw through Binkle's trick very well indeed, but he knew that everyone would pretend he had washed off the picture, for no one would want to own up to how stupid they really *had been* in saying Binkle's empty canvas was a lovely picture.

'No one's ever to *mention* that picture again!' exploded Herbert Hedgehog, bristling with rage.

No one ever did – except Binkle and Flip, and they *would* keep saying what a pity it was to have destroyed Binkle's lovely blue sky *and* Herbert Hedgehog's portrait.

'And who would have thought,' said Binkle to Flip that night – 'who *would* have thought that silly old pretend-picture could really show us how stupid everybody in Oak Tree Town was! All of them thought they were so clever, yet nobody was clever enough to see through my little trick! Dear, dear, Oak Tree Town isn't very good at telling the truth! But we *have* had some fun out of it!'

And they certainly had.

Chapter 4
Bing-Bong, the Paw-Reader

Flip and Binkle had been good for a week and three days, and Binkle was beginning to find things very dull.

'Oh!' he moaned. 'Can't we find a more exciting job than delivering medicine for Sammy Squirrel the chemist? I hate carrying baskets of bottles every day.'

Flip preferred to be good. He was afraid of Binkle's exciting ideas; they nearly always led to trouble.

'It's a *very nice* job,' he said anxiously. 'For goodness' sake don't give it up, Binkle.'

Binkle put on his cap and opened the door of their home, Heather Cottage.

'Come on!' he said crossly. 'I won't give up the job – not until we get a better one, anyway!'

The two rabbits ran across Bumble Bee Common on their way to Oak Tree Town. When they got there, Binkle saw a big notice pinned up outside Dilly Duck's at the post office. He crossed over to look at it. In big letters it said:

```
A GRAND BAZAAR WILL BE
HELD IN OAK TREE TOWN
```

Binkle stroked his fine whiskers and began thinking. 'Come on,' said Flip, pulling him next door into Sammy Squirrel's. 'Don't dream like that, Binkle. It's time we began work.'

But all that day Binkle went on thinking, and hardly said a single word to Flip. In the evening, when Sammy Squirrel paid him, Binkle gave Flip a dreadful shock.

'We shan't be here tomorrow,' he said, 'so I'm afraid you must get someone else to do the job.'

'Oh, Binkle!' cried Flip in dismay. 'Whatever do you mean?'

'Sh! I've got a lovely idea!' said Binkle,

pulling Flip outside. 'Come on, and I'll talk to you about it.'

'I don't like your lovely ideas,' wailed Flip.

'You'll love this one,' said Binkle. 'Listen. Did you read that notice about the bazaar outside Dilly Duck's?'

'Yes,' said Flip. 'What about it?'

'Well, at that bazaar there's going to be Bing-Bong, who can read all your life in your paw,' said Binkle excitedly. 'He'll tell you what's going to happen to you in the future, too.'

'Bing-Bong! I never heard of him,' said Flip. 'Anyway, what's it to do with us?'

'Oh, Flip, *can't you guess? One of us will be Bing-Bong,* and read everyone's paws!' said Binkle excitedly.

'Binkle! How can you be so silly?' gasped Flip. 'You *know* we can't read paws!'

'Well, we don't need to, silly!' grinned Binkle. 'We know all about everyone in Oak Tree Town, don't we, and we can easily tell them all about themselves. They won't know us, for we'll be dressed up and they'll think we're wonderful!'

'But how can we tell them what will happen in the future?' asked Flip.

'We'll make it up!' said Binkle. 'Oh, Flip, what fun it will be!'

'Will it?' said Flip doubtfully. 'But look here, Binkle – you're to be Bing-Bong. I don't look a bit like a Bing-Bong person. You do; you're so fat and big, and you've got such lovely whiskers.'

Binkle twirled them proudly.

'Yes, I shall be Bing-Bong,' he said, 'and you can be my assistant. First I must write a note to Herbert Hedgehog, who's getting up the bazaar.'

He sat down and got pen and paper. Presently he showed a letter to Flip. This is what it said:

> *Bing-Bong Castle.*
>
> *Dear Sir,*
> *I am Bing-Bong, the reader of paws. I am pass-*
> *ing through Oak Tree Town on the day your*
> *bazaar is held. I will call there and read paws.*
> *Yours faithfully,*
>
> *Bing-Bong.*

'There!' said Binkle proudly. 'What do you think of that?'

Flip's nose went nervously up and down as

he read the letter.

'I do hope it will be all right!' he sighed. 'You *do* have such extraordinary ideas, Binkle. I don't know how you think of them.'

The letter was sent, and when it reached Herbert Hedgehog he was most excited. He at once arranged to have a little room set apart in Oak Tree Town Hall for Bing-Bong to sit in and read paws.

'It *will* be grand,' he said; 'and my, won't lots of people come to the bazaar!'

Binkle and Flip were very busy making clothes to wear. Binkle wore a purple suit with a red cloak wound tightly round him. On his head he wore a pointed hat with red stars painted all over it. He looked very grand.

Flip was dressed in baggy trousers and a little black velvet coat. He didn't like them much, for he felt he looked rather silly.

At last the day came, and the two rogues set out over Bumble Bee Common.

'Now, remember!' said Binkle. 'Call me Your Highness, and bow before you speak, Flip. You take the money and keep it safe. Leave the rest to me.'

Flip wished he could leave *everything* to Binkle, and not go at all, but he didn't dare to say so.

'Oh my! There's Herbert Hedgehog waiting to greet us outside the town hall!' he whispered. 'Do you think he'll see through our disguise, and know it's us?'

'Of course not!' snapped Binkle, striding forward. Herbert Hedgehog bowed very low when he saw the red-cloaked visitor.

'This is His Royal Highness Bing-Bong!' stammered Flip nervously.

Herbert stood all his prickles up very straight and made way for the two rabbits to go in.

'Very good of you to come, Your Highness,' he said, and led the way to the little room at the back of the hall. 'I've made this room ready for you. We shall love to have our paws read by the wonderful Bing-Bong.' And he bowed again.

Binkle looked round when Herbert had gone out.

'I'll sit in that big chair,' he said. 'You stand by the door, Flip. Charge twenty-pence a time, remember.'

Very soon there came a timid little knock. Flip swung the door open. Outside stood Creeper Mouse.

'Please, I've come to have my paw read,' he said nervously, holding out twenty-pence.

'Your Highness! Someone to have his paw read!' called Flip, beginning to enjoy himself.

Binkle put on some big spectacles and glared at Creeper, who stood tremblingly looking at him. He knew Creeper very well, for he was the postman of Oak Tree Town.

'Come here,' commanded Binkle, 'and hold out your paw.'

Creeper put out his tiny little paw. Binkle stared and stared at it.

'Your paw tells me many things,' he said. 'It tells me that you have five brothers and sisters. You are married, and you –'

'Oh! Oh! Oh!' squeaked Creeper, lost in wonder. 'How clever you are! It's quite true. Does my paw really tell you that?'

'Of course it does,' answered Binkle. 'Don't interrupt. It tells me that you walk miles and miles every day, carrying a heavy bag.'

'Yes, yes, I do,' squeaked Creeper. 'What's in the bag?'

'Your paw will tell me,' said Binkle solemnly, bending closely over it. 'Let me see – yes, you carry letters. You are a postman.'

'Well, did you ever!' exclaimed the astonished mouse, swinging his tail about delightedly. 'Oh, Bing-Bong, please tell me what will happen in my future.'

Binkle looked at his paw again. 'You will go on a long journey, in a ship,' he said gravely. 'You will carry letters all your life. You will have twenty-nine children.'

'No, no!' shrieked Creeper in horror, snatching his paw away. 'Twenty-nine children! Why, how would I feed them all? Oh! Oh! Twenty-nine children!'

And he rushed out of the room before Binkle could say another word.

Flip began giggling, but Binkle told him to be quiet.

'Sh!' he said. 'Creeper will be telling all the others at the bazaar, and in a minute they'll all want to come and have their paws read. Hark! There's someone now, Flip.'

It was Herbert Hedgehog, holding out his twenty-pence and looking rather nervous.

'Creeper Mouse says you're wonderful, Your Highness,' he said to Binkle. 'Could you read my paw, please?'

Binkle looked at it solemnly.

'You live in a yellow cottage,' he said. 'You grow very fine cabbages.'

'So I do – so I do,' said Herbert, in the greatest astonishment.

'You have many friends,' went on Binkle, 'but the two who love you best are – '

'Who?' asked Herbert eagerly, wondering if they were Dilly Duck and Sammy Squirrel.

'They are – Flip and Binkle Bunny!' said Binkle, now thoroughly enjoying himself.

Flip's nose went up and down in delight, when he saw the astonishment on Herbert's face.

'My best friends!' echoed Herbert. 'Flip and Binkle Bunny! Well, well, well! I must be nicer to them in future.'

'I *should*,' said Binkle, twirling his whiskers very fast, to hide the smile on his face.

'Tell me some more,' begged Herbert. 'Tell me about the future.'

'Er – if you dig up your biggest cabbages, you *may* find a pot of gold underneath,' began Binkle.

'Fancy! Oh, my goodness! Oh, excuse me!' begged Herbert, almost stuttering with

77

excitement. 'Pray excuse me! I *do* want to go home straight away and see if I can find that gold.'

'Oh no, don't do that,' shouted Binkle in alarm . . . but Herbert was gone.

'Bother!' said Binkle in dismay.

'What did you want to go and say such a silly thing for?' demanded Flip. 'You *know* there's no gold under his old cabbages.'

'Sh! There's someone else,' whispered Binkle, as a knock came at the door.

It was Wily Weasel the policeman! Flip almost fell backwards in fright.

'May I have my paw read?' asked Wily politely.

'Oh – er – yes!' stammered Flip, wishing to goodness he could run away.

Wily went up to Binkle and bowed. Binkle took hold of his paw and glared at it. He didn't like Wily Weasel, for Wily had often scolded him and locked him up for being naughty. 'Your paw does not tell me nice things,' he began. 'It tells me that you are always hunting people and being unkind to them.'

'I have to be,' said Wily Weasel cheerfully. 'I'm a policeman! There are lots of rogues about Oak Tree Town, and I have to punish them!'

Binkle decided to change the subject. 'You are married,' he said, 'and you love to smoke a pipe.'

'Quite right,' said Wily, in a pleased voice. 'Now tell me about the future. Shall I get rich?'

'*Never*!' said Binkle firmly. 'You'll get poorer and poorer. You'll lose your job. You'll be hunted away from Oak Tree Town. You'll be put in prison. You'll –'

'Ow!' yelled Wily in terror, as he listened to all the awful things Binkle was telling. 'Don't tell me any more! I don't want to hear anything else!'

He went hurriedly out of the room, groaning and sighing.

'Ooh, I *did* enjoy that,' said Binkle. 'That's made up for a good many scoldings I've had from Wily.'

Thick and fast came the knocks on the door, and Binkle was as busy as could be, telling everyone about themselves. As he knew all their pasts and made up their futures, he enjoyed himself thoroughly – till in walked someone he *didn't* know!

He was a badger. He held out his paw to Binkle and waited.

'Er – er – er –' began Binkle. 'You live far away from here.'

'No, I don't,' said the badger. 'I live in the next town.'

'That's what I meant,' cried Binkle. 'Er – er – you are married.'

'I'm not!' said the badger indignantly. 'You don't know what you're talking about! You're a fraud!'

Just at that moment there came a great hubbub outside the door and it burst open suddenly. Herbert Hedgehog came stamping in, followed by a whole crowd of others.

'I've pulled up all the lovely cabbages in my garden,' he wailed, 'and there's not a piece of gold anywhere! And all my beautiful cabbages are wasted! You're a fraud, Bing-Bong – that's what you are!'

'Yes, he is,' cried the badger. 'Why, he told me I was married, and I'm not!'

Wily Weasel strode up to Bing-Bong and glared at him.

'Are you Bing-Bong, or aren't you?' he demanded. 'We're all those awful things true that you said were going to happen to me – or not?'

'Oh! Oh!' wept Flip. 'They weren't true, Wily, he made them up, truly he did!'

Wily turned round and looked at Flip and grabbed off his peculiarly-shaped hat.

'Oho!' he said. 'So it's Flip Bunny, is it? And I suppose Bing-Bong is our own friend Binkle?'

Binkle decided to make the best of it.

'Yes,' he said, 'I'm Binkle. I only came to the bazaar to give you a bit of fun. I'm sorry about your cabbages, Herbert. Flip, give him the money you've got. He can buy some more.'

Everyone stared in astonishment at the

red-cloaked rabbit. They could hardly believe it was Binkle who had read their paws. They had so believed in him. For a minute everyone felt angry and probably Flip and Binkle would have got into trouble – if Creeper Mouse hadn't begun to laugh.

'He told me I'd have twenty-nine children,' he squeaked. 'Oh dear! Oh dear, and I believed him!'

Then everyone began laughing, and even Wily Weasel joined in.

'I'll let you off *this* time,' he said to Binkle.

82

'But next time – you just look out! Go off home, both of you. Give Herbert your money to buy more cabbages – and don't let me hear any more of you for a long time!'

Flip and Binkle scampered off to Heather Cottage as fast as they could go, very thankful to get off so easily.

And for two weeks Binkle had no more lovely ideas. After that – well you'll see!

Chapter 5
Binkle and Flip
Try to be Good

Binkle had got into trouble so often that he was beginning to be rather tired of it. He was seriously thinking of turning over a new leaf and trying to be good for a change. But he very much wondered what Flip would say.

He decided to tell him that night as they were getting ready for bed.

'Flip,' he said solemnly, 'what about being good for the rest of our lives?'

Flip brushed the hair on his big ears and sniffed scornfully.

'Don't try to be funny,' he said.

'But I mean it,' said Binkle, rather cross with Flip's sniff.

Flip stopped brushing and stared at Binkle

in surprise.

'But you *couldn't* be good, Binkle!' he said, at last.

'I jolly well could, then!' cried Binkle indignantly. 'I tell you I'm tired of being naughty, and playing tricks on people. I'd like to be good and kind to them for a change. I'd like to go and visit poor old Mowdie Mole, who's got a cold, and I'd like to take Dilly some of our flowers, and –'

'And go and dig up all Herbert Hedgehog's garden for him, and wash up

Wily Weasel's breakfast things?' suggested Flip, giggling.

'Oh well, if you're going to be *funny*,' said Binkle offended, 'I won't say any more. But you just wait till tomorrow morning.'

Flip thought he would. He couldn't understand Binkle's fit of goodness, and he wondered if he had eaten too many carrot-tops at supper. He rather hoped Binkle *would* still feel the same in the morning, because Flip, too, was getting rather tired of being naughty. He was really a harmless little bunny, who much preferred the quietness of being good to the excitement of being naughty.

Binkle might probably have woken up in his usual energetic, don't-care spirits if he hadn't had an awful dream. He woke Flip to tell him about it.

'Listen, Flip,' he said. 'I dreamed I went to Bess Bunny and played a trick on her. I dreamed I took Bobs Bunny and Bimbo Bunny, her twins, and left two big turnips wrapped up in their cradle instead, to give her a fright. Then I took Bobs and Bimbo home, and when I got home, what do you think?'

'What?' asked Flip.

'They'd both turned into little fox cubs!' said Binkle.

'Ow!' said Flip, who hated foxes, big and little.

'That's not the worst,' said Binkle. 'They began to grow and grow and *grow* in my arms till I dropped them – and they were full-grown foxes! And they said, "Binkle, you shall be punished for your badness," and one of them ate me up! Oh dear, dear!' And Binkle shivered at the thought.

Flip shivered too. 'What did the second fox do?' he asked.

'He ate *you* up,' answered Binkle solemnly.

'Ow!' said Flip again, and disappeared beneath the bedclothes. Binkle thought he would too, and together the poor bunnies trembled under the blankets.

'It shows we'd better be good,' whispered Binkle, after a time.

'Yes,' agreed Flip in a muffled voice. 'Take your ear out of my mouth, Binkle, and sit up and look if we're safe.'

Binkle began to feel better, and bravely sat up. The sun was streaming into the bedroom and he began to laugh.

'It's all right,' he said, 'let's get dressed. We'll go straight down to Mowdie Mole's and offer to read to her while she's in bed with her cold.'

So the two rabbits dressed quickly and went down to Mowdie Mole's. They knocked at the door and waited.

No answer.

They knocked again. Still no answer.

'Mowdie Mole,' called Binkle, 'we've come to read to you.'

Not a sound came back to them in answer.

'Dear, dear!' said Flip anxiously. 'Do you suppose she's too ill to answer us, Binkle?'

'I expect she is,' said Binkle. 'It's a mercy we came along. We can get her breakfast, perhaps. Won't that be a kind thing to do, Flip?'

'Yes,' agreed Flip, wondering if Mowdie Mole would let them share her breakfast.

'Look here,' said Binkle, 'that window's open up there. Let me stand on your back and I'll climb in. Then I'll open the door to you, Flip.'

In half a minute Binkle was inside Mowdie Mole's house, and let Flip in too. They went and listened outside Mowdie's door.

'I *think* I can hear her breathing,' said Binkle. 'She must be asleep. It would be a nice surprise for her if we got her breakfast ready without telling her, and took it up, wouldn't it?'

Flip thought it was a fine idea, and the two rabbits went to the kitchen. They found some milk and put it on the fire to boil, and Binkle thought he could make some nice soup of onions, carrots, and potatoes. So he got them all out and began cutting them up.

Suddenly they heard footsteps outside, and then the front door opened!

'Who *can* it be?' gasped Flip in fright.

They soon saw – for who should come walking straight into the kitchen but Mowdie Mole herself! She nearly fell down in astonishment when she saw Binkle and Flip cutting up onions and carrots in *her* kitchen.

'Binkle! Flip! What *are* you doing?' she demanded.

'We thought you were ill in bed!' said Binkle, feeling very small.

'Ill in bed!' snorted Mowdie Mole. 'You

thought nothing of the sort! You knew I was out shopping, so you thought you'd come and help yourselves while I was gone. I didn't think you were quite as bad as *that*, Binkle Bunny!'

'We're *not*!' said Flip indignantly, finding his tongue, 'We really thought you had a cold and were ill in bed – so we're getting your breakfast to take up to you. We're trying to be good!'

'Trying to be good,' laughed Mowdie scornfully – 'when everybody *knows* you never have been! You want scolding, and I'm going to do it! The idea of messing up my nice kitchen like this!'

She pounced on Flip – when sizzle-sizzle – sizzle! The milk in the saucepan boiled over.

'Oh, my nice clean stove!' wailed Mowdie, and ran to take the sauce pan off the fire.

Binkle and Flip took to their heels and ran out of Mowdie's kitchen like a streak of lightning. They didn't stop running till they were back at Heather Cottage.

Then they sat down and looked at each other.

'It's hard to be good and kind,' said Binkle sorrowfully.

'But we mustn't give up,' said Flip. 'You won't, will you, Binkle?'

'Not *just* yet,' agreed Binkle. 'We'll take Dilly Duck a big bunch of our best pink roses next, I think. She *will* be so pleased. Come and pick them, Flip.'

They picked two great bunches of roses, and, each carrying one, they walked down to Oak Tree Town, feeling very kind and generous. Just as they got to Herbert hedgehog's, Binkle stopped.

'Look!' he said to Flip, pointing to Herbert's side gate. 'Herbert's left it open. Let's go and shut it for him, Flip, in case any thieves get in.'

The two bunnies went into the front garden and slammed the side gate. Then they turned to go out again – and whom should they meet coming in but Herbert Hedgehog!

He stared at them in surprise.

'Good morning, dear Herbert,' said Binkle politely. 'We just saw your side gate open, and shut it for you.'

Herbert looked even more surprised.

'Stuff and nonsense!' he said rudely. 'Never heard of you shutting anyone's gate for them before. No, you've been picking my roses – that's what you've been doing, you pair of rascals!'

'We *haven't*!' said Binkle indignantly. 'We picked these out of our own garden!'

'And what did you mean to do with them?' asked Herbert disbelievingly.

'We're taking them to Dilly Duck as a little present,' said Flip.

'Taking them to – Oh, ha, ha, ha!' roared Herbert. 'Never heard of you giving anyone a present before, Binkle. Ha, ha, ha! And *my* roses, too!'

'They're *not* your roses,' stormed Binkle. 'Come on, Flip, let's go before this silly old hedgehog makes us angry.'

Herbert stopped laughing.

'If you go out of my gate, I'll call Wily Weasel,' he said. 'He's just over there, and I'll tell him how I saw you coming out of my side gate with bunches of roses to take to Dilly Duck. Do you think he'll believe you?'

Binkle thought Wily Weasel most certainly would *not* believe them, and he grew very angry.

'*Take* the roses, then,' he shouted, and banged the whole bunch down on Herbert

Hedgehog's head. Flip did the same, and before the surprised hedgehog could call for help, the two bunnies dashed out of the garden and were far away up the road.

'*Well*!' choked Binkle in great disgust. 'That's the last time *I'll* ever try to be good! All our roses wasted!'

Flip mopped his hot nose with his big red

handkerchief and smoothed back his floppy ears.

'Let's try just once more,' he begged. 'People say the third time's lucky, you know. And everybody says it's hard to be good, so it's no wonder *we* don't find it very easy, is it, Binkle?'

'Well, what's the use of being good if people only think we're being naughty?' demanded Binkle crossly. 'You can go on being as good as you like, Flip. I've *stopped*.'

Binkle sat down by the roadside and fanned himself. Flip sat down too, and tried to make Binkle change his mind.

But Binkle wouldn't. He pushed Flip away and settled himself comfortably to have a nap.

'Go and be good somewhere else,' he said. 'You're disturbing me.'

Flip wriggled his nervous little nose in despair. Then he looked down the road, for he heard footsteps.

It was Brock Badger carrying a large and heavy sack.

'Look, there's Brock Badger,' said Flip. 'He's got a sack. Let's go and help him, Binkle.'

Binkle snored hard.

'You'll hurt your throat if you do that,' said Flip 'I know you're not asleep. Come and help Brock, Binkle. He's limping.'

'Snore, snore!' went Binkle as loudly as ever he could.

'All right,' said Flip crossly. 'I'll go and be good by myself.'

He got up and went down the road to meet Brock Badger.

'Good morning,' he said. 'Is that sack heavy? You seem to be limping!'

'I've got a thorn in my foot,' said Brock.

'Well, let me carry your sack home for you,' offered Flip, in his kindest voice. 'Then your foot won't hurt so much.'

Brock stared at him in surprise.

'No thanks,' he said. 'I know your tricks, Flip. You'd run off with my sack, and I couldn't catch you with my bad foot.'

'I *wouldn't*,' cried Flip. 'I'm trying to help you.'

'H'm, that's a new idea,' said Brock disbelievingly.

'Perhaps you haven't heard,' explained Flip, 'Binkle and I are trying to be good now. At least, Binkle's a bit tired of it, but I'm not.

Let me help you, Brock Badger.'

'All right,' said Brock, seeing that Flip really did mean what he said. 'Very kind of you, I'm sure. Catch hold.'

He gave the sack to Flip, and together they went up the road. They passed Binkle, who was lying just where Flip had left him.

'Snore, snore!' he went, as they passed.

'Being good seems to have tired him out,' remarked Brock. 'I don't wonder. It must have been very difficult for anyone so *dreadfully* naughty as Binkle.'

Now, Binkle wasn't really asleep – only pretending – and he distinctly heard what Brock said to Flip. It annoyed him very much.

He opened one eye just as they had passed him. And he saw something that nearly made him sit up with delight.

The sack Flip was carrying was full of carrots. It had a hole at the bottom, and Binkle saw a long red carrot drop quietly out in the road.

In a second he jumped up. He ran into Heather Cottage, which was just near by, and caught up a sack of his own. Then he ran back to the road.

There lay the carrot! Flip and Brock

weren't in sight, for they had turned a corner.

Binkle picked up the carrot and popped it into his sack. Further on lay another one, and he picked that up too, and ran on again to a third one.

When he came to the corner, he peeped round it. He could see Flip and Brock in the distance, plodding along not knowing anything about the hole in the sack. He waited till they had turned another corner, then on he went again, picking up the dropped carrots quickly and popping them into his sack with a chuckle.

'Carrots don't seem to stay long with good people' he laughed.

Flip and Brock were going along talking. At first Flip found the sack very heavy, but soon it seemed to feel lighter.

'I must be getting used to the weight,' he thought, and padded along happily, thinking how nice it was to be good.

Brock began to think Flip wasn't such a bad bunny after all.

'I'll give you six of my carrots when we get home,' he promised. 'It's very nice of you to carry my heavy sack.'

'Oh, it's not a bit heavy,' said Flip truthfully. Quite half the carrots had fallen out by this time, though neither Flip nor Brock knew it. Binkle was picking them all up, and *his* sack was not nearly so light as it was at first. He was very careful to keep well out of sight, for he had no intention of being caught.

At last Flip and Brock reached the Badger's house. Flip took the sack off his shoulders and put it on the ground. There seemed to be something the matter with it. It looked very thin and empty.

Flip and Brock both stared at it.

'*Where are my carrots?*' roared Brock suddenly, catching hold of Flip's collar.

'Don't, Brock!' cried Flip. 'Look, there's a hole in your sack! They must have tumbled out!'

'You did it on purpose, so that you could go back and pick them up,' shouted Brock, shaking Flip until his ears flapped his nose.

'I *didn't!*' he cried indignantly. 'Come back with me along the road and get them. They'll all be there, you'll see!'

So Brock and Flip went back to the road – and, to Flip's enormous astonishment, not a single carrot could he see, even though he went right back to where he started. He really couldn't understand it.

'Are you *sure* there were carrots in your sack?' he asked Brock.

Brock bristled all over with rage, and

made a pounce at Flip and caught him by the fur of his neck.

'*Carrots!*' he snorted. 'Of course there were! Now I'm going to shake you, you wicked little rabbit!'

Flip gave one tremendous yell of fright, jerked himself away from Brock, and ran to Heather Cottage as fast as ever he could. Brock was left behind with a handful of fur and a bad temper.

Flip rushed into Heather Cottage and banged the door. He went into the kitchen and sat down, trembling, on a chair.

Binkle was there, and he looked rather surprised to see Flip come in in such a hurry.

But Flip was even more surprised than Binkle when he saw what was on the floor – for there stood a large sack of carrots!

He stared at them as if he couldn't believe his eyes.

'Oh-oh! There's Brock's carrots,' he groaned.

'No *my* carrots,' said Binkle. 'I found them. And finding's keeping.'

'It isn't, when you know the owner,' said Flip. 'If it hadn't been for you picking up the carrots that dropped out of the sack, I wouldn't have got a sore neck. Brock's pulled half my fur off.'

'Serves you right,' said Binkle. 'I told you you ought to have stopped trying to be good.'

This was too much for Flip. He jumped up in a fury, caught hold of Binkle's collar and jerked him to his feet.

'It's your naughtiness that made my kindness no use,' he stormed. 'Come on outside. I'm going to give you such a shaking that the dust will fly. Grr-rrr-rr!'

He ran Binkle outside into the garden and shook him and twisted him till his arm ached. Binkle struggled and fought and at last got free. He ran indoors.

'All right,' he said, 'I'll have all the carrots – see!'

But, oh, my goodness! No sooner had he got indoors than he stood and stared in fright. For Brock, who had been listening outside the window, had jumped in, got the sack of carrots, and jumped out again. He put his head in the window and made a face at Binkle.

'I shook Flip, and Flip shook you,' he grinned. 'so you've both had a good shaking, which is what you deserve! And I've got my carrots back, and a new sack. Thank you very much, Binkle Bunny.'

He ran round the garden and bumped into Flip. He took out a big carrot and gave it to him.

'Here you are,' he said. 'It wasn't your fault. Go and tell Binkle what you've got for being good. It was nice to see you shake him till his teeth rattled!'

Off he went chuckling, with his sack on his back.

And when Binkle looked out of the window and saw Flip sitting down comfortably, eating a very large carrot, he was very annoyed indeed.

But Flip looked so terribly fierce that Binkle really didn't dare to ask him for even a bite. So he went to bed instead, which is the best place really for bad bunnies.

Chapter 6

The Whistling Biggle-Boggle

Oak Tree Town was terribly upset. Little Bobs Bunny had disappeared the week before and nobody knew where he had gone to. And now Minny Mouse, one of Creeper Mouse's little daughters, had gone.

'What *can* have happened to her?' wailed Creeper in despair.

'And what *can* have become of poor little Bobs?' sighed Bess Bunny, his mother.

Sammy Squirrel came up and joined the group.

'I think I know what has become of him,' he said sadly. 'I am afraid that family of Polecats who have just come to live near Bramble Dell have had a great deal to do with the disappearance of Bobs Bunny and

Minny Mouse.'

'Oh dear, dear!' said Dilly Duck. 'I never *did* like Polecats!'

'What can we do about it?' asked Herbert Hedgehog.

'Let's go and tell Wily Weasel and see if he knows what to do,' suggested Mowdie Mole.

The others thought that was a very good idea, and soon everyone trooped off to Wily's.

He was very concerned about it.

'But it's no good, I can't do anything,' he said. 'We don't know for *certain* that Pippit and Pinkie Polecat have caught Bobs and Minny. The only thing I can suggest is that we think of some idea to make the Polecats go away.'

Just at that moment Flip and Binkle Bunny strolled up. Wily Weasel saw them.

'Hi, Binkle!' he called. 'Come here a minute.'

'What for?' asked Binkle nervously. 'I haven't done anything naughty for *ages*.'

'Well, here's a chance to put your brains to work to some good use,' said Wily. 'You're always having ideas of some sort – ideas that lead you into trouble. Now, if you can think of an idea to make Pippit and Pinkie Polecat go away from Bramble Dell, we should all be very grateful to you!'

Binkle began to smooth his long whiskers and perk his ears up. He felt very proud to have Wily Weasel talking to him like that.

'Well, young Bobs Bunny was my favourite nephew,' he said, 'and to punish Pippit Polecat for catching him, I will certainly think of some idea. Meet me at my Uncle Rob the Rabbit's shop tomorrow, and I will have a wonderful idea all ready to tell you.'

Then he took Flip's arm and marched away with him, leaving the people of Oak Tree Town gaping after him in admiration.

'Flip and Binkle Bunny aren't always good, but they *are* clever,' said Dilly Duck, who hadn't many brains herself, and knew it.

'They're more mischievous than bad,' said Bess, Binkle's sister. 'Well, well! We shall see if Binkle has thought of an idea by tomorrow.'

All the folk at Oak Tree Town went home and waited anxiously for the next day.

Binkle shut himself up in his bedroom, and thought and thought and thought.

Presently a smile came over his face and his nose twitched. He opened the bedroom door and called out to Flip.

'Hi, Flip!' he shouted. 'Do you know what a Biggle-Boggle is?'

'A Biggle-Boggle!' exclaimed Flip in astonishment. 'No, I don't. What is it?'

'Ha! ha!' chuckled Binkle, disappearing into the kitchen and getting paper and pen out of a drawer. 'You'll know soon enough, Flip.'

And not another word would the provoking Bunny say. He just sat in the kitchen and wrote something that he wouldn't let Flip see.

Next day he and Flip went down into Oak Tree Town and walked into Rob Rabbit's shop. Everyone was there waiting for them in Rob's big room at the back.

'Good morning,' said Binkle cheerfully. 'Hope I haven't kept you waiting.'

'Have you thought of an idea?' demanded Wily Weasel.

'Yes, I have,' answered Binkle, 'and if I can't get Pippit and Pinkie Polecat away from Bramble Dell in a day or two, I'll cut off my lovely whiskers!'

'Tell us your idea, quickly!' begged Sammy.

'Well, listen,' said Binkle, carefully shutting the door and lowering his voice.

Then in the middle of a breathless silence he began to tell them his plan.

'First of all, I want this notice I've written out to be copied and pasted all over Oak Tree Town and Bramble Dell,' he began, and he spread out the notice for them to see. It was a most peculiar one:

<u>LOST</u>
A WHISTLING BIGGLE-BOGGLE
Dangerous to
POLECATS and FOXES
If Found, Please Return to Grunzle,
at Oak Tree Town Hall

'A Biggle-Boggle!' gasped everyone. 'What's that?'

'And who's Grunzle?' asked Sammy Squirrel.

'Flip is,' explained Binkle, to Flip's immense astonishment.

'Oh, *am* I!' exclaimed Flip. 'And what are *you* going to be?'

'Never mind that,' said Binkle. 'You'll know sooner or later. All you've got to do is to sit in the town hall and pretend you're waiting for a Biggle-Boggle to turn up.'

'Tell us more about your plan,' said Sammy, who was beginning to see what Binkle was going to do.

'No,' said Binkle firmly. 'I shall tell nothing else, in case somehow or other it leaks out and everything's spoilt. You must leave the rest to me. There's only one thing to remember. If anyone asks about Biggle-Boggles, say they're very dangerous.'

The others had to be content with that, and each of them promised to copy out one of the notices and paste it up. Then they all went home.

Next day all over Oak Tree Town appeared large notices about the lost Biggle-Boggle. An extra large one was pasted up in Bramble Dell, where Pippit and Pinkie Polecat often went for walks.

Flip Bunny went to the town hall, dressed like a showman. He had blue trousers, a red coat, a bendy hat, and fine tall boots. He felt very proud of himself indeed.

Binkle didn't appear. He had gone off by himself with a penny whistle, and wouldn't tell Flip anything. He was thoroughly enjoying himself.

'Now, mind!' he said to Flip before he went. 'Just you remember every single thing I've told you about Biggle-Boggles, Flip.'

Well, Flip hadn't sat in the town hall very long before there was a great commotion in the street outside, and Pippit Polecat rushed into the hall.

'Are you Grunzle?' he asked Flip. 'Well,

what's this about Biggle-Boggles? What are they?'

'They're fat creatures,' explained Flip, remembering all Binkle had told him. 'And they love to dance in the moonlight among the trees and whistle to the moon. They live in China, generally.'

'Well, how did this Biggle-Boggle come *here*?' demanded Pippit, who didn't like the sound of them at all.

'I brought it back from China,' said Flip calmly. 'I'm a showman, I am!'

'You've no *business* to bring Biggle-Boggles back from China,' scolded Pippit. 'Why are they dangerous to Polecats and Foxes? Aren't they dangerous to anyone else?'

'Oh, *no*!' answered Flip, pretending to be astonished. 'They're very fond of everyone except Polecats and Foxes. But they have two favourite meals – one is fried Fox's brush, and the other is stewed Polecat-tail. That's why I put that bit about danger in my notice. I shouldn't like my Biggle-Boggle to be put in prison for catching you and eating your tail.'

'Oh my!' said Pippit in dismay. 'Nor should I! I do hope it won't come anywhere near our home.'

He went off sadly, wondering what to do about it. No sooner had he got home and told his wife all that Flip had said, than he heard something which made him jump and turn pale from his whiskers to his tail.

It was a peculiar whistling sound! It came from the trees just beyond their house.

'Oh!' gasped Pinkie, 'it's the Biggle-Boggle! Pippit! Whatever shall we do?'

'It won't come *here*!' said Pippit bravely.

'Cheer up! I'll go and tell Grunzle later on that his Biggle-Boggle is near here, and perhaps he'll come and catch him.'

When at last the whistling stopped and Pippit thought everything was safe, he rushed once more into Oak Tree Town and went anxiously to Flip.

'Your Biggle-Boggle's near our house,' he said. 'We heard him whistling. Come and get him.'

Flip stood up and put on his hat. He walked off with Pippit till they came to Bramble Dell. Then he pretended to search and search, but nothing did he find except – Binkle!

'Have you seen anything strange about here?' asked Flip, pretending not to know Binkle.

'Yes, a peculiar fat creature that whistled,' said Binkle. 'He asked me if I knew of any Polecats round about here.'

'Ow! ow!' shrieked Pippit, and dashed into his house at once and slammed the door.

Flip and Binkle went off giggling. Pippit came no more to the town hall that day.

But that night, when he looked fearfully out of his bedroom window, he heard a whistling noise again. And there, dancing in the moonlight among the trees, he saw what looked like a peculiar fat creature!

'Oh, dear, dear! It's the Biggle-Boggle!' he said in terror. 'Whatever shall I do? I must certainly get Grunzle to catch him tomorrow.'

After a time the Biggle-Boggle stopped dancing and whistling, and disappeared among the trees, and Pippit and Pinkie went shivering to bed.

Next day Pippit went to Flip again and told him what he had seen.

'Do come and catch him!' he begged.

Flip looked grave.

'I don't think I dare,' he said. 'When he starts dancing like that it means that he's made up his mind to have one of his favourite meals. I daren't catch him till he's had it. He might bite *me*!'

'Oh dear!' groaned Pippit. 'Whatever are we to do?'

'Cheer up! He'll be all right when he's had stewed Polecat-tails,' said Flip cheerfully.

Pippit howled in despair and rushed out of the hall, pulling his whiskers in the greatest alarm.

Nothing more was heard of him that day and Flip got rather tired of doing nothing. But when evening came, Binkle walked jauntily into the town.

'Hullo! Aren't you playing at being the Biggle-Boggle?' asked Flip.

Binkle didn't answer.

'Call the folk of the town together,' he commanded.

Flip did so.

'Come with me,' said Binkle, when they were all there, and he led them to Bramble Dell.

He stopped just near the Polecats' cottage and pointed.

'Look,' he said.

They all looked. A big notice was hanging from a tree in the garden:

THIS COTTAGE TO BE LET

it said!

'It's empty!' said Binkle. 'Pippit and Pinkie Polecat have gone away for good.'

'Hurrah! hurrah!' shouted the folk of Oak Tree Town. 'Three cheers for Binkle and the Biggle-Boggle.'

And they hurried Binkle and Flip back to the town as fast as they could. In half an hour Mowdie Mole and Dilly Duck had got a lovely feast ready in the town hall, and Wily Weasel told Binkle to sit at the head and Flip at the foot.

Didn't they feel proud!

And at the very end, Wily Weasel stood up and said: 'We are very glad that Binkle and Flip Bunny have done Oak Tree Town a good turn at last. I hope they will never be naughty any more.'

But I'm afraid that was rather too much to hope for.

Chapter 7
Binkle Gets a Dreadful Shock

Binkle and Flip had nothing to eat. Their larder was empty, and they were dreadfully hungry.

'Nobody will give us any work,' sighed Binkle. 'They all seem cross about something or other.'

Flip looked very gloomy.

'*Nobody* wants us,' he said. 'I've a good mind to go out and get lost and never come back. Perhaps Oak Tree Town would be sorry then.'

Binkle sighed – then he frowned – then he chuckled, jumped up and slapped Flip on the back.

'Binkle, *don't* do that!' said Flip angrily. 'I keep telling you not to. And if it means you've got an idea, just keep it to yourself. Flapping and slapping about like that!'

'But Flip, this is *your* idea,' began Binkle. 'I think if you went out and got lost, and then got captured by some foxes, who said they wouldn't let you go unless we gave them cabbages and things, I'd get Oak Tree Town to give them, don't you see?'

'No, I don't see at all,' answered Flip crossly. 'I'm certainly not going to be so silly as to get captured by foxes.'

'No, not *really*,' said Binkle excitedly. 'You could go and hide somewhere, Flip, and I'd write letters to Herbert and all the others, saying you were captured by foxes who wanted food to let you go. I'd collect the food and pretend to take it to the foxes, and you'd come along home and we'd eat it all ourselves.'

Flip, seeing that he wasn't *really* to be captured by the foxes, thought it wasn't such a bad idea.

'I'll go straightaway and hide now in the old hollow oak tree in Cuckoo Wood,' said Flip. 'You must hurry up with your letter writing, Binkle, because it's not very comfortable there, and I shan't want to stay there too long.'

'I'll write the letters now,' said Binkle. 'Goodbye, Flip! Come out of the oak tree when you hear me whistle.'

Flip scuttled off, climbed into the hollow tree, and settled down.

Binkle wrote three letters – one to Herbert Hedgehog, one to Wily Weasel, and one to Sammy Squirrel. They were all the same.

> *We have captured Flip Bunny, but we will let him go free if you will give six cabbages, six lettuces, and six turnips to Binkle Bunny to bring to us tomorrow afternoon in Cuckoo Wood in exchange for Flip.*
>
> *With kind regards from*
>
> *Three Foxes.*

'There!' said Binkle, licking the envelopes with his little pink tongue. 'There! Now when Wily, Herbert, and Sammy give me the things, I'll pretend I'm taking them to the foxes, but really I'll go and whistle to Flip, and when he jumps out of the oak tree, we'll have a jolly good feast.'

He popped the letters into Wily's, Herbert's, and Sammy's letter boxes that night, then back to Heather Cottage he went, and got into bed, chuckling to think of the cabbages, lettuces, and turnips he and Flip would have next day.

When Herbert and Sammy read their letters that night they went straight to Wily

Weasel, the policeman, about it, and found him frowning over the letter Binkle had left in *his* letter box.

'What *shall* we do?' said Sammy. 'We can't let poor little Flip remain a prisoner.'

'We must be sure and give Binkle Bunny the cabbages and things tomorrow to set Flip free,' said Herbert.

Wily Weasel frowned harder.

'I'm very worried,' he said. 'I think I shall go up to Cuckoo Wood myself tonight, and warn anyone I see there that bad foxes are about, in case anybody else gets captured.'

He put his helmet over his sharp ears, and went out, leaving Sammy and Herbert to talk over their letters.

It was very dark in Cuckoo Wood and nobody was about at all. Wily went along, quietly whistling to himself, thinking about poor Flip Bunny.

Suddenly, to his enormous astonishment, he heard a voice just by him say: 'Is that you, Binkle?'

Wily stopped and looked round. He swung his lantern here and there, but nobody was lurking among the trees. He leaned against a big oak tree and waited. He heard nothing and began to think he must have been mistaken. He pursed up his whiskered mouth, and began quietly whistling again.

'*Binkle!*' said a voice so close to him that he jumped. A head poked out of the hollow oak tree and a nose sniffed into his ear. 'Why have you come whistling round here tonight? Have you brought any cabbages?'

'Oho!' thought Wily to himself, as he recognised Flip's voice, 'so those letters were all a trick of Binkle's. Oho!'

He suddenly turned, caught hold of Flip's collar and swung him out of the tree on to the ground.

'Now!' he said, flashing his lantern on to the astonished rabbit, 'just tell me what you're doing here, Flip?'

Flip was too surprised to answer for a moment. He had quite thought it was Binkle he had heard whistling to him. He couldn't think *what* to say!

'I – I've been captured by foxes,' he stammered at last.

'Oh, *have* you?' snorted Wily disbelievingly. 'Well, why didn't you escape?'

'I – I – didn't think of it!' said poor Flip. 'Binkle's going to rescue me tomorrow.'

'Well, I'm going to rescue you instead,' said Wily, 'and you're going to come along with me. I see through the trick you and Binkle have played, and I'm going to play a little trick on Binkle while you're safely locked up in Oak Tree Town.'

He tied Flip's paws together, and roped him to a tree. Then he felt for a pencil and his notebook. He wrote a note and pinned it on the tree. This is what it said:

Ha! Ha! We have really *captured Flip, and when he's fattened up, we'll eat him. Thank you for him, Binkle. If you want him back,* perhaps *we might exchange him for twenty cabbages, twenty lettuces, and twenty turnips. Come tonight and see.*

From Three Fierce Foxes.

'That'll give Binkle a shock!' grinned Wily. 'When he reads that he'll think you really *have* been captured, Flip. I wonder what he'll do!'

Flip was too miserable to answer. Wily unroped him and together the two went through the wood to Oak Tree Town, where Wily locked Flip safely up for the night.

After that he went to see Herbert and Sammy, and with many chuckles told them what he had done.

'We'll give Binkle a regular fright tomorrow,' he laughed. 'And mind! When he comes begging for cabbages and things, don't give him any, and tell everyone else not to, either. Binkle must have a proper punishment this time.'

Next morning Binkle thought he would pop up to the hollow oak tree in Cuckoo Wood and tell Flip he had written and delivered the letters.

So off he went, gaily humming to himself. he whistled as he came near the oak tree, expecting Flip to pop his head out. But he didn't.

'Perhaps he's asleep,' said Binkle. Then he caught sight of the notice Wily had pinned up and he went to read it.

'Oh! Oh! Oh!' he yelled when he had read it. 'Flip's really been captured. Oh! Oh! Oh! What shall I do? Poor, poor Flip! Oh, those horrid foxes! Oh, I must really go and beg for twenty cabbages, lettuces, and turnips. Oh my! Oh my!'

He peeped in the hollow tree and saw it was empty. Then, with flapping ears and staring eyes, he raced through the wood into Oak Tree Town.

He saw Mowdie Mole and Sammy Squirrel in Herbert Hedgehog's front garden. Breathlessly he rushed up to them.

'Oh!' he cried, 'Flip's been captured by foxes. They say they'll eat him unless we take them twenty cabbages, turnips, and lettuces.

Oh, quick, Herbert, let me dig up some of yours?'

'Certainly *not*,' said Herbert. 'My cabbages are much too valuable.'

'You horrid thing!' cried Binkle. '*You'll* give me some of yours, won't you, Sammy and Mowdie!'

But Sammy and Mowdie refused, too.

'No,' they said, 'certainly not.'

Binkle couldn't believe his ears. How could anyone be so unkind when poor Flip was captured by foxes?

He rushed to Dilly Duck's and begged her for some of her lettuces.

'No, Binkle,' said Dilly, who was usually the soul of kindness. 'I can't spare any today.'

'Oh, *please*, Dilly?' begged Binkle. 'Just to save Flip!'

'If Flip and you were good bunnies,' began Dilly, 'perhaps I might have given you some. But you're not!'

'Oh, I'll always be good now, I'll always be good,' cried Binkle. But it wasn't any use, Dilly wouldn't change her mind.

Binkle went to Susie Squirrel and to Derry Dormouse, to Riggles Rat and to Wily

Weasel, and to everyone else he knew. But not one single person would let him have any cabbages, lettuces, or turnips.

'This is my punishment for being naughty,' sighed poor Binkle. 'Oh, dear, dear! To think poor Flip's been captured like that, all because I had a naughty idea. Oh, if ever I get him back, I'll never be bad again, never!'

He sat on the ground and thought what he could do for Flip. He frowned hard and two tears flopped on to the ground.

'I know!' said Binkle at last. 'I'll go to the tree myself tonight, and offer to go with the foxes in exchange for Flip's freedom. I'm fat and plump and they'd much rather have *me*.'

So the brave little bunny got up and ran off. On the way he met Wily Weasel, who wanted to know where he was going, and Binkle told him. Wily said nothing and went on his way, leaving Binkle to go to the oak tree.

But Wily was thinking hard. He was astonished that Binkle should have thought of giving himself up for Flip, and he was very pleased. He hurried into Oak Tree Town and called on all the folk there, telling them what Binkle was going to do.

'Binkle's braver and better than we

thought, for all his naughtiness,' said Wily. 'If only we could persuade him to be good and use his clever brains to help us instead of playing tricks on us, he would be of great use to Oak Tree Town.'

'What are you going to do about Flip?' asked Herbert.

'This is what I've planned,' said Wily with a chuckle. 'We'll all go up to Cuckoo Wood with Flip. When we see Binkle there, I'll call out as if I were a fox, and ask him questions. We'll see how he answers them, and if he answers properly, we'll loose Flip and let him go back to Binkle.'

So off they all went, taking poor frightened Flip with them. Wily hid behind a tree directly he saw Binkle and waved the others away.

Binkle was standing there alone, looking about for the foxes.

'Foxes!' he called, 'foxes!'

'Yes!' answered Wily, making poor Binkle jump in fright.

'I haven't got the things you wanted,' said Binkle in a trembling voice. 'So I've brought myself. Will you have me instead of Flip? I'm much fatter.'

'Are you a good or a naughty bunny?' asked Wily, still pretending to be a fox.

'A naughty one,' answered Binkle, 'but I wish I hadn't been, for then I wouldn't have got Flip into trouble.'

'Do you want to be good now?' asked Wily, thoroughly enjoying himself, and grinning at all the others listening.

'Yes, I do,' answered Binkle, 'and I'll promise to be good always if only you'll let Flip go free.'

Wily turned to the others.

'Do you hear that?' he whispered. 'We'll

let Flip go to him, and then we'll tell him we'll keep him to his promise.'

Flip's paws were untied and he scampered to Binkle, who could hardly believe his eyes and hugged him as if he would squeeze him to death.

Then to his tremendous surprise all the others came crowding up.

'Now, Binkle!' said Wily, 'we've heard your promise, and we don't mean you to break it. You must always be good now you've got Flip back again.'

Binkle stared in amazement.

'Is it all a trick?' he asked at last.

'It's a trick that came out of *your* trick,' said Wily, and told him all that had happened.

Binkle was too thankful to know that Flip really was safe, and that he himself wasn't going to be captured by foxes, to say anything cross or unkind. He really *did* feel he'd never be naughty again and, of course, if *he* wasn't, Flip wouldn't be.

Sammy Squirrel kindly asked both bunnies to go to supper with him, and as they were really too hungry for anything, they went.

That was just six months ago, and as far as

I know, Binkle has kept his word. But I am told he is already beginning to find it rather a nuisance to be good. So I shouldn't be at all surprised to hear that he and Flip have become bad bunnies once again.

I hope not, but if they do, you may be sure I'll let you know.

Good Bunnies

And now there's nothing left to say
Except
    Fare-
        Well,
Because I've told you all the tales there
Are
    To
        Tell,
And Oak Tree Town is peaceful now, for
Flip's
    Quite
        Good,
And Binkle is behaving as a
Nice
    Bunny
        Should!

Mowdie Mole is very pleased,
Because,
    She
        Says,
She never did approve at all of
Such
    Bad
        Ways.
And Dilly Duck and Susie Squirrel
Both
    Agree
        Too,
And Derry says he really can't
Believe
    It's
        True!
Herbert Hedgehog says he'd rather
Wait
    And
        See
A little while, before he asks the
Pair
    To
        Tea,
He wants to be quite sure that Binkle
Means
    What

He says,
And does his really-truly best to
Mend
    His
        Ways!
Wily has a lazy time, he's
Grown
    Quite
        Fat,
He often calls on Binkle for a
Nice
    Little
        Chat,
And on the shady garden seat they
Both
    Sit
        Down,
And talk about the latest news in
Oak
    Tree
        Town.
Sammy Squirrel's pleased to find they're
Both
    So
        Nice,
He's been to supper with the bunnies
Once

Or
      Twice.
They both were neat and tidy from their
Toes
      To
           Their ears,
And Sammy said they hadn't looked so
Nice
      For
           Years!
But soon a day is sure to come when
Binkle
      Will
           Say,
'Flip, I've thought of something naughty!
Hip,
      Hip,
           Hurray!'
And in his eyes will shine again that
Bright
      Old
           Twinkle –
And then I'll tell *another* tale of
Bold
      Bad
           Binkle!

Happy Days Enid Blyton

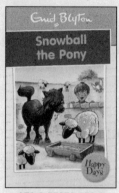

Enid Blyton
Snowball the Pony

978-0-75372-578-8

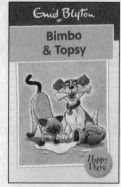

Enid Blyton
Bimbo & Topsy

978-0-75372-579-5

Enid Blyton
Run-About's Holiday

978-0-75372-581-8

Enid Blyton
The Adventures of Binkle & Flip

978-0-75372-580-1

Enid Blyton
Binkle & Flip Misbehave

978-0-75372-582-5

Enid Blyton
Shuffle the Shoemaker

978-0-75372-584-9

Enid Blyton
Merry Mister Meddle

978-0-75372-583-2

Enid Blyton
Mister Meddle's Muddles

978-0-75372-585-6

Enid Blyton
Mister Meddle's Mischief

978-0-75372-586-3

Enid Blyton
You're a Nuisance Mister Meddle

978-0-75372-577-1

Enid Blyton
The Adventures of Mr Pink-Whistle

978-0-75372-587-0

Enid Blyton
Mr Pink-Whistle Has Some Fun

978-0-75372-588-7

Enid Blyton
Mr Pink-Whistle's Party

978-0-75372-589-4

Enid Blyton
Mr Pink-Whistle Interferes

978-0-75372-590-0

Enid Blyton
Hello Mr Twiddle!

978-0-75372-591-7

Enid Blyton
Mr Twiddle in Trouble Again

978-0-75372-592-4

Enid Blyton
Don't Be Silly, Mr Twiddle

978-0-75372-593-1

Enid Blyton
Well, Really, Mr Twiddle!

978-0-75372-594-8

RIDDLES SERIES Enid Blyton

Follow the daring Nick and his sister Katie as they solve mysteries, elude kidnappers, discover treasure, and much more.

978-0-75372-554-2

978-0-75372-547-4

978-0-75372-555-9

978-0-75372-561-0

978-0-75372-562-7

978-0-75372-563-4

FAMILY ADVENTURES

Enid Blyton

Follow these families as they discover the joys and perils of growing up, find new adventures, and set the world to rights.

978-0-75372-548-1

978-0-75372-558-0

978-0-75372-559-7

978-0-75372-564-1

978-0-75372-557-3

978-0-75372-560-3